THE PREACHER'S MAIL-ORDER BRIDE

Mail-Order Brides of Sweet, Texas, Book Two

ELIZABETH CHASEN

The Preacher's Mail-Order Bride

Copyright © 2017 Elizabeth Chasen

ALL RIGHTS RESERVED

CHAPTER ONE

Mrs. Ambrosia Mulberry hustled toward the church, late for the weekly quilting club meeting. In her hurry, she rounded the corner and ran smack into Pastor Andrews! Thanks to her ample figure, she bounced right off the poor young man and managed not to squash the box of cherry scones she was carrying.

"Oh my goodness to heaven," she declared, trying to catch her breath. She did indeed love all things sweet and her padded figure showed that well enough. Today it had come to her rescue.

Pastor Andrews steadied her with a hand to her arm. "Mrs. Mulberry, forgive me, I wasn't watching where I was going. Are you all right?"

She chuckled and waved off his worries. "Oh yes, yes, I'm fine. Here, thankfully my treat for you was not flattened in our little calamity." She thrust the hat box at him. It was filled with the cherry scones he loved. Instantly, she was rewarded by his startlingly beautiful smile. That smile was beautiful—there simply was no other way to describe it. Handsome was not an adequate enough description. And what it did to his eyes, the way they crinkled up at the edges, well, it just brought joy to her old heart to see it.

"Mrs. Mulberry, if you're out to make me into a portly pastor then I'm on to your plan but unable to resist the temptations of your baking genius."

She chuckled as he pulled a scone from the box right then and there and popped it into his mouth. He sighed. "Pure bliss."

Ambrosia felt a bloom of satisfaction at the pastor's praise. Her sweet husband had loved her baked goods and it was nice to see others enjoy them.

Especially the young preacher, who she thought should have a sweet young wife to bake for him instead of her. But still, she took joy in baking him a weekly batch of treats. It was the least she could do for the man of God—it was her ministry, in a way.

Still, she couldn't help pointing out the truth to him once more. "You need a wife, Pastor Andrews. Someone who can bake and cook to your delight. *And* be there at your side in your ministry."

It was true and quite often the main topic of conversation at the quilting club meeting. The man gave and gave and never complained as he went about the Lord's work with action and not just words. If someone was sick, he went and milked their cows for them and chopped their wood. Or whatever else needed doing. He was always looking out for everyone else and then went home to a lonely, dark house and probably a cold supper.

Why, the ladies of the quilting club had even considered sending off for a mail-order bride for him. Especially after the recent excitement in town when a young mail-order bride had shown up in town to marry the sheriff. It was quite exciting to realize first that she was a mail-order bride and second to find out that the sheriff had not sent for her! It was still a mystery to everyone as to who had sent for her. And it was a miracle that things had worked out to their benefit.

Thrilled by the entire event, the ladies had discussed it but in the end hadn't had the courage to go through with sending off for someone for the sweet pastor. Still, she could hope.

Why, it would have been a huge uproar considering everyone in town was still reeling from the fact that they had someone in their midst who was actually sending off for brides. And everyone wanted to know who the *mystery cupid* was, as they'd nicknamed the culprit.

The ladies were convinced that if the mystery cupid would do it once, she or he might very well do it again. They hoped so at least.

All the ladies had denied being the cupid, but that didn't mean all manner of townsfolk hadn't blamed it on them. Which, by most standards and stories they'd heard of the towns that had been sending off for mail-order brides, many ladies' quilting clubs or other town matrons had done so. But not her friends here in Sweet, no sir—not them. But if not them, then who?

The cupid was smart. Why, the sheriff and his new bride were living in wedded bliss since Lucy had come to town. The mix-up that had, thankfully, turned out good. Now Ambrosia wondered who would be next. Because her intuition told her that it was going to happen again.

And soon.

Suddenly, there was an uproar behind her and she spun to see the rambling stagecoach racing into town. The horses' hooves thundered on the ground as the driver snapped the whip and yelled for folks to get out of his way. He didn't pull up on the leathers until he was in front of the feed store where he normally stopped. He was still yelling as the coach slowed.

"I need the doctor!" barked the grizzly old driver. "The stage's been robbed and I've got a passenger who's been shot!"

Ambrosia gasped and Pastor Andrews thrust the scones at her. "Hold these, please." He then raced to offer aid.

Mrs. Mulberry clutched the box as she hurried after him and prayed whoever was inside that stagecoach would survive.

Jarred Andrews said a prayer as he raced across the rutted road to the stage. The driver had been smart, bringing it to its regular stopping point in front of Big John Wiggins' feed store because the doctor's office was on the side street around the corner. Jarred reached the stage just as the driver swung the door open.

"She's a tiny thing," he snapped. "But she's tough. I never seen anything like her, standing up to that bandit the way she done. Why, she told that bandit he couldn't have what she had in her bag and when he tried to take it, she walloped him on the head with a metal rod she had hidden under her skirt. He was so mad, he shot her."

"He shot a lady?" Jarred couldn't believe the crook had shot a woman. He entered the stagecoach and found her crumpled on the floor, where she'd probably fallen off the seat when the driver raced over the rough terrain to get her here. There was blood everywhere.

Thankfully, the blood was coming from her shoulder and not some other more vital area of her small body. She was young. Young and spunky, evidently, if she'd smacked the no-good upside the head with a metal rod. Amazed, Jarred quickly stripped off his shirt to try to stop the bleeding. He pressed hard and she groaned, but he kept the pressure on the wound. He'd learned when he'd been in the war that bleeding needed pressure to stop it. And despite this being her shoulder, she was losing a lot of blood.

"What can I do?" Big John looked in over the driver's head. The big man was tall enough to look over most everyone's head.

"Get the doctor," he demanded.

"Doc's not there," Big John said. "But I can open the office for you. Want me to carry her?"

The doctor wasn't in. The knowledge sank over Jarred with dread. "No, I'll carry her. Get the door open."

He gathered her in his arms and lifted her from the stagecoach floor. She cried out and her eyes flew open and met his.

Jarred's heart thundered as he gazed into eyes the color of the first blue streak of a morning sunrise. He faltered. "Hang on," he told her then moved forward as gently as he could.

She groaned, closed her eyes and went limp again.

It was for the best at the moment.

"Hold the stage for the sheriff," he told the driver.

"I sure will. Take care of her," the driver grunted. "Never seen nothin' like it."

Jarred understood the stagecoach driver's admiration but he wished the young lady had done what the robber had told her to do. She might not be in this shape if she hadn't rebelled. "I'll do my best. Big John, where is the doc?"

"Delivering a baby out at the Murrys'," the big man said. "But I'll send for him to come back as soon as he can. Come on, lets get her to the doc's office and do what we can."

Jarred followed him as his thoughts spun. He had

tended to more bullet wounds than he wished to remember and he didn't want to do it again. He'd done it because the military had thrust him into it and he'd seen more death and pain than he cared to remember. But he had to help her.

Big John had the door open by the time he strode around the corner to the doctor's office. He carried the woman inside and crossed to the examination table, where he gently placed her.

She groaned and her eyes flickered open again. She mumbled something and he didn't understand. She tried again and he leaned close so he could understand.

She whispered, "He didn't get it, did he?"

"Get what?" Jarred tried to hold her down as she struggled, causing the wound to bleed more. "Please, you have to stop struggling."

"No. Did he get my purse?" she gasped, finally giving out and laying back on the table, breathing hard.

He put pressure on her wound. "I don't know if he got it. I wasn't there. But right now, we have to get your shoulder to stop bleeding. You've been shot."

"But my purse." She groaned. Her pain-glazed

eyes held his and then she passed out again.

Jarred couldn't move, was frozen for a moment. Mesmerized by her. *Help her.* He shook himself. He had to stop the bleeding. "Get Mrs. Mulberry. I need her." He glanced at Big John.

"I'll get her." Wasting no time, he hurried from the room.

Jarred lifted her up slightly and was relieved to see that the bullet had made a clean exit. "Thank you Lord." He shot a glance heavenward, thankful he wasn't going to have to dig a bullet out of her shoulder. Thoughts of the war hit him; he forced them from his mind and focused on saving her.

He had just torn the material of her dress away from her shoulder when Mrs. Mulberry entered the room, huffing and puffing as she rushed over to him.

"I'm here! I'm here. What do you need me to do? Oh, the dear girl. This is just horrible."

"I'll need you to help me. Can you heat up some water? And it's been awhile since I was here when Doc was working on someone. You'll need to find me the antiseptics. Luckily, the bullet made a clean exit so we just need to stop the bleeding until Doc gets back. Hopefully soon or I'll need to stitch her up."

"You can do that?" Mrs. Mulberry gasped.

He hadn't told anyone that in the war he'd been pulled in to assist the doctors when they were overwhelmed. "I learned in the war. Pray that she stays knocked out and if she wakens, I'll need you to help calm her. We won't want the bleeding to start back up. Can you do that?"

"I can do that. As you know, my sweet husband required a lot of care before he died. It was not pleasant. I learned that my stomach is impenetrable and I can do anything I set my mind on."

Yes, this was true. Her poor husband had been in a terrible accident and had to have his leg removed before he finally passed away. It had been a horrible, horrible thing and Mrs. Mulberry had had to help take care of the wounds. Sadly, despite all their efforts, Mr. Mulberry had been overcome with infection and had suffered before he'd passed away.

Poor woman. Jarred had always had deep respect

and admiration for her because of her continuing trust in the Lord and cheerful disposition. The fact that she never gave up her hope and dedication to the Lord was inspiring. She was somewhat meddlesome but a blessing to this town and greatly admired by him and others. The fact that she made cherry scones that were straight from heaven, was, as far as he was concerned, a blessing that he looked forward to each and every week.

Especially hard weeks. It was amazing how much he looked forward to that little box of sweets.

And like today, she would always tell him that one day he would have a wife who could make cherry scones because she would teach her. *"You just need to get a wife,"* she would declare.

He would always chuckle and tell her that when the Lord saw fit, he would bring him the wife that he intended for Jarred to have.

However, he was beginning to wonder whether the Lord, with his busy schedule, had forgotten about him needing a wife. The wife Jarred had begun to long for more and more.

He worked quickly and his thoughts locked on the wife the Lord would eventually bring him. He knew exactly the qualities becoming a pastor's wife. One who was already patient and kind, organized, mature…maybe older than he was.

She needed to be… His gaze locked on the poor young lady he was working on. She was probably in her twenties, a few years younger than him and far too young, too inexperienced and spunky. Definitely not the type of woman he would need.

Why was he thinking about this right now anyway? He pushed the thoughts out of his mind and said a prayer for the Lord's help.

Moments later, he got the blood stopped and the shoulder bandaged up. He hoped the doctor would arrive soon.

Mrs. Mulberry patted him on the shoulder. "You did a fine job, Pastor. This young woman will forever be in your debt. I'm proud of you. But shouldn't she have regained consciousness by now?"

"It may just take awhile. She's been through a trying ordeal. Maybe she'll wake up soon."

As if on cue, her eyes fluttered open and locked onto him.

His pulse jumped like a bucking horse and his mouth went dry. *Dear Lord, she was beautiful.*

CHAPTER TWO

Gabby Anson hurt. As she woke up, she stared into the eyes of an angel. The man had a long face with a straight nose and soft, brown eyes full of compassion.

"Try not to move," the angel urged. "I know you're in pain but you don't need to start bleeding again. You're pale—you've lost so much blood already."

Angel—no, the man, she corrected herself knowing that her brain was muddled and that he was really a man. She thought about the robber who tried to take her purse. "That no-good scoundrel tried to take my purse." Her thoughts were confused and she felt weak as she tried to keep her focus. The man began to spin in front of her and his smile faltered as he spun.

"Easy now. You've been hurt but you're going to be okay. Everything's going to be fine."

His voice was soothing; she nodded and then realized he hadn't answered her question. "My purse?" she asked again.

An elderly lady looked over the man's shoulder and smiled brightly. "I will go look inside the stage. Don't fret, dear. I'll be right back."

Gabby relaxed, then fought the pain in her shoulder.

The woman patted her arm. "Hang in there. I know you're hurting. Big John, come in here while I'm gone in case you're needed," she told the man outside the door.

A large man came inside. "I'm here if you need me," he called to the doctor.

"Thank you, Big John."

Gabby knew they were all trying to help her but

all she could think about was what the robber might have taken. Everything she had to start her life here was in that purse.

Worse, she'd betrayed her father by taking money from his stash in his office. But she'd had to do it…but now, it very well could be gone.

The very thought distressed her. She gasped and felt a tear streak from her eye. She'd taken the money and was so ashamed, but despite what her mother and dad wanted, she just could not marry Alfred and so she'd resorted to being a thief—just like the man who'd shot her.

It was awful, but Alfred…the idea of being married to him for the rest of her life just wasn't right. He was a nice man and came from a nice family. It was just that the more she thought about the marriage, the more hemmed in she had become. When her maid had told her that she'd written to a man in the West and was going to become a mail-order bride but couldn't go through with it and wasn't going to go the next morning, Gabby had grabbed at the chance to escape her own troubles and had taken Laura's place on the train out of St. Louis and then the stage. She'd had a plan, but if her money was gone...what would she do? Really become a mail-order bride? Panic seized her and she struggled to sit up.

"Hold on, you need to rest. You've lost a lot of blood and are pale and weak. Please relax."

She slumped back onto the table. He gently rubbed her arm, trying to calm her. *He was so nice. And so handsome...*

"You've had a terrible ordeal. Facing an outlaw and defending yourself, I'm told," he said, his voice soothing. "You're very brave."

Gabby relaxed. Her shoulder seemed to not hurt as much while he rubbed her arm. "I never thought I'd face an outlaw," she managed. Never even considered meeting one. But then again, all she'd been thinking about was escaping a life of misery, married to a man she could never love.

And now, if she were broke, she might very well have to resort to doing that very thing here in the wilds of Texas.

This handsome doctor had no idea that asking her

to be calm was impossible. And yet his touch was luring her to do just that.

Suddenly the door opened and a big man entered, along with the lady. She hustled over with alarm on her face. "I'm so sorry," she said. "Your purse wasn't on the stage."

Gabby groaned. "My money was in my purse."

The doctor looked sympathetic. "I'm sorry about that. Hopefully the sheriff can get it back. But right now you need to lie back down. Mrs. Mulberry, is there any sign that the doctor is getting near?"

Gabby did as he asked because she had no fight left in her. *What was she going to do?*

The older woman—Mrs. Mulberry, he'd called her—came to her side and patted Gabby's arm. "I'm so sorry, you dear girl. Where were you heading? I'm sure that we as a town can come up with your fare to help you get where you were going."

"Is this Sweet, Texas?"

"Yes, it is," Mrs. Mulberry said.

The older man moved forward to look over her shoulder, his brow crinkled. "What are you coming here for? We don't get female visitors very often."

She looked at him and felt her pulse increase as he picked up her wrist and felt her pulse. She wondered whether he could tell that her pulse was racing. By the way his eyebrows cinched together, she thought he might. "I'm…" She paused. *Could she say the words? What options did she have?* She had had the money as a safeguard but now she wasn't sure whether she had any other options.

"I'm here to marry the pastor. Jarred Andrews."

The doctor's expression was one of alarm. He let go of her wrist and stepped back.

Mrs. Mulberry gasped and Big John leaned forward to look over the doctor's shoulder at her. The big man's eyes had widened considerably at her news. And she thought she saw a smile on his face before he hid it quickly.

"Did you say Pastor Jarred Andrews?" the doctor asked after a moment.

"That's what I said. Pastor Jarred Andrews. I wrote him letters. He's expecting me." She tried not to feel guilty for the small lie because it was actually her friend, Laura, who had written to him. "I'm sure you know him, Doctor."

"No, I'm not the doctor. I'm the pastor and I didn't send for a wife."

"You-but...you saved me. I would have bled to death." Her head was fuzzy again. *What did all this mean?*

"He saved you because he knew how. But he is the pastor," Mrs. Mulberry said. The delight in her voice was completely evident and more confusing to Gabby.

"She's right," Big John vouched, smiling too. "This here is Pastor Jarred Andrews. The doc was out delivering a baby."

"Oh..." she said, confused by the confusion on her rescuer's face. He'd said he hadn't sent for a bride. "But...what does this mean? I don't feel well."

"I'm not sure. What's your name?" the doctor who was really the pastor asked.

She stared at him and tried to comprehend what

this new revelation meant for her. "I'm Gab—I mean I'm Laura Tyson." The lie felt horrible to her. She had stolen money from her father and now she was lying to a preacher. The good Lord was surely frowning down on her right this very minute. She was in so much trouble and coming here had been a huge mistake.

CHAPTER THREE

Jarred was completely baffled. Who had done this? Immediately, he thought of the sheriff, his friend Trey Jones. Not even a month ago, a mail-order bride arrived for him. And he hadn't sent for her. It was the same situation because Trey hadn't known anything about it either.

It seemed that the matchmaker, whoever it was, was at it again. This was a dilemma.

Just a couple of weeks ago, he and Trey had had this very conversation. Trey had found him sitting on his back porch and Trey had asked why he never married. There are a lot of reasons why he never married. One was that the Lord hadn't sent him a wife. And he kept saying that when the time was right, the Lord would send him the right woman. But not because of a matchmaker. *Who could it be?*

Jarred's thoughts rolled. But all the while, the beautiful Laura Tyson—whose pale expression didn't sit well with him—blinked at him with her big eyes, as if she couldn't believe what he had said. Then she grimaced and reached for her shoulder. The pain was probably radiating through her. He reacted by touching her arm, needing to comfort her.

"Relax," he urged. "We'll get this figured out." He wasn't sure how but he didn't want to distress her more than she already was right now. She had been through a horrible ordeal and now to find out she'd come here on false pretenses was terrible.

"Yes, we will." Mrs. Mulberry had a smug, if not happy, expression on her face, though she was trying hard to hide it.

Was she the culprit, the matchmaker?

Big John had his arms crossed and stood calmly,

his lip hitched slightly on one side. There was a glint of humor in his eyes. *What was that about?* There was nothing funny about what was going on. Everyone respected Big John. He owned the feed store and he gave good advice and was always helpful. *Did he see something good in this situation that Jarred had missed?* Right now Jarred needed advice.

The pastor in him could not let this poor woman hang in the balance. He looked at Mrs. Mulberry. "Could you stay with her, please? I need to check on a few things. I'll be right back."

"I'd be happy to stay. You go do what you need to do and we will be just fine."

He looked at Laura. "If you'll excuse me, Mrs. Mulberry will take good care of you. I'll be back."

His mind wasn't working as he hurried to the door, hoping he didn't look as if he were running away. He just needed a moment. When he reached Big John, he paused. "May I have a word with you, please?"

"Sure can, preacher." The older man followed him out into the sunshine.

Jarred gulped in the fresh air, hoping it would clear his head. The poor woman in there had come all this way to marry him. *How could that be?* He raked a hand through his hair and met Big John's watchful gaze. There was definitely a smile on his face.

"Why are you smiling? I'm completely at a loss about what to do. Who would send for a mail-order bride for me? I did not send those letters. Do you have any advice? Because I could sure use some."

Big John sobered, his expression thoughtful. "Well, preacher, you seem like a man who is mighty lonely to me. Maybe you can marry her. She did come all this way."

"Marry her? Is that all the advice you have? I don't know her. I didn't send for her. Someone in this town has put me in the same predicament that they put Trey in. And it is highly unfair to that unfortunate woman inside the doctor's office."

"Looks to me like it turned out pretty good for the sheriff. That man is happier than a pig in slop."

Jarred cringed. "I will admit that he's happy. I'm not so sure I would say he was as happy as a pig in slop nor would I know for sure if he wanted to be that kind of happy. But yes, he is very happy and so is his bride. But that still doesn't answer my question or fix my dilemma. I'm a man of the cloth. What would my congregation think if I married a total stranger when I hadn't even sent for one? That someone else in this town had decided to do it for me? It's really put me in a bad spot."

"Well, none of that answers the question on you being a lonely man who could use a female to help you out in your ministry. You give too much, you work too hard and then you go home and spend all your evenings alone. Maybe whoever did this thought it was time for you to have someone. Maybe they, like they did with Trey, tried to find someone suitable for you."

Jarred thought about that. "My needs for a wife and a companion are long and complicated. I have to have someone well-suited for the ministry. Someone mature. Someone suited to handle the problems that come with the ministry. The list goes on, and you and I both know that the female in that room in there is far too beautiful, far too young, and I have a feeling

27

maybe far too gullible considering she came all this way. No, she is not suited for what I need in a wife."

Big John frowned. "I'm not sure why being beautiful would disqualify her. Or young. You are not all that old yourself, Pastor. And to me, that she traveled all this way means she has courage to face uncertain situations. You sure are assuming a lot."

Jarred stiffened. "I'm coming up on thirty this year. I assumed, or think that when I do marry, that my wife should be probably at least twenty-eight years of age. Clearly, she has to be barely twenty."

"Hold on, preacher. I heard you say many times that when the good Lord decided to send you a wife that's the one you would marry."

"But the good Lord didn't send this one to me. Somebody—I don't even know who it is—sent her to me."

"Well, last time I checked, the Lord works in mysterious ways. Couldn't he use someone in town to do his work?"

Jarred was completely skeptical about that. "I believe that if the good Lord wanted to send me someone, he wouldn't have to use a matchmaker to do it. Or a nosy person who thinks they know best for everyone."

His curiosity was getting the better of him. *Could it be the quilting ladies at the church? Maybe Mrs. Mulberry was in on this.* She always told him he needed someone. Had told him once more just before the stage rolled in today. Had she gotten tired of waiting on the Lord and taken matters into her own hands? "Well, I'm not marrying her. And now she says she's been robbed and has no money." He frowned at that. "She has no money. What will she do? Will she go back home? I don't even know where she came from."

Big John looked concerned now. "That is a dilemma. These are hard times. Most of these mail-order brides, from what I understand, don't have anything in the first place so the fact that she had a little money is shocking. Maybe you'll need to help her out, Pastor. I mean, you're the pastor after all."

Jarred closed his eyes momentarily. He *was* the pastor. Just because this was personal didn't mean he could walk away from someone in need. He would have to help her find lodging. And then he would have to help her either find work or a way to get back home.

He saw the doc's carriage come around the corner. A sense of relief washed over him. At least the doc was here. At least there was something positive about the day. He looked at Big John. "You're right. I'll help her find some place to stay, maybe Miss. Claira's."

"Maybe that would be a thought, or maybe Mrs. Mulberry might have a spot for her. She did let on that she might be willing to keep her and not charge her anything. I know as a pastor, funds are a little lacking."

"That is true," Jarred said. That was another reason why he wasn't married. As a preacher, he wasn't a wealthy man. He didn't even own the home he lived in. It was part of the deal that came in being the pastor of the church.

"I'll speak with Mrs. Mulberry. Thank you. That's a very good suggestion and I have a feeling that she'll be quite amicable to it."

He hoped she would. Because after she left here, she would need someone to care for her wound when the doctor couldn't do it. And Mrs. Mulberry was very good at that. She was the perfect choice. So, after speaking with the doctor, they entered the building and he said a prayer that the good Lord would show him the way and that everything would turn out okay. And he prayed that this poor girl, who'd come all this way thinking she was going to get married, would not be too disappointed when she learned that he was not going to marry her.

Ambrosia decided that whoever this matchmaker was, she liked it. She had been praying—and praying—for the good Lord to send Pastor Andrews a wife. And now here was this darling young woman who, she thought, would be just perfect for him. Now, of course, she had seen on his face that he was having none of it. It would be a shock. She remembered how shocked the sheriff had been when that little lady had gotten off that stagecoach who came to town to marry him, all because of this unknown matchmaker answering letters, corresponding with these little ladies and pretending to be the sheriff—and now the pastor. Of course, it was actually very terrible. Deceitful even. But if the good Lord was overlooking it, she approved wholeheartedly.

Looking at the young lady now, she said, "So you traveled all this way to get married. You are such a brave young woman. You will be interested to meet the sheriff's wife, Lucy Jones. She'd tell you that she also traveled all this way to be a mail-order bride. And I was surprised, too. Though the beginning was a little rocky, they are doing so wonderful. They are so happy. So this is just exciting to me. Not that you're hurt or injured or you had to endure such a horrible thing. I'm thinking that you probably won't be getting married right away."

"He said he didn't send for me. I don't know what to do."

"There, there—we will get this figured out, so don't panic. The pastor will do the right thing. And he needs a wife."

Laura paled. "But he didn't send for one."

Being a pastor made it hard for him to find a wife.

What with all the visiting friends and neighbors all across the county and preparing sermons and tending to the sick and the poor…he had no time for courting. And then again, Sweet, Texas hardly had any females. What females they had were just a lot of widows in the quilting club.

No, this was the perfect solution. Ambrosia decided right then and there that she might not have started this but she was jumping on board with whoever this Good Samaritan in town was. She would help as much as she could to fan those flames…if there were any.

And she hoped there were.

She beamed. "Since you've been hurt, I propose that you come to my house. I live right here in town. I lost my poor husband years ago and before he died he was in a terrible way. He had wounds that needed to be cared for, so I'm quite proficient at taking care of wounds. When the doctor arrives, he will vouch for this. See, you would be in quite capable hands. And it's just me and that big house and I would adore some company while you recuperate before your marriage.

In reality, that will give you a little time for you and the preacher to get to know each other a little better. What do you say?"

She waited and said a prayer that the young woman agreed.

Gabby stared at the little lady. If her shoulder didn't hurt so bad, she would've hugged her. She wouldn't be out on the street and could hopefully come up with a solution. She was so glad Laura hadn't come only to find out she had been duped. Mrs. Mulberry was offering her the chance to recuperate and time to get her thoughts together.

"Thank you so much, Mrs. Mulberry, for your kind offer. I'm so grateful. I don't know what I would do without you."

"That's wonderful, just wonderful," Mrs. Mulberry exclaimed just as the door of the doctor's office opened and the preacher entered. And behind him, the large man they called Big John. There was a small man with a lot of wrinkles carrying a black bag who came in with him. He was bald on top and hustled in a no-nonsense manner, set the bag down and strode her way. He bypassed the preacher and then John and Mrs. Mulberry moved out of his way. *This must be the doctor.*

"Well, I hear you have had an accident. You had some excitement and that a robber shot you. I don't know that I've ever treated a female who's been shot by robber. You're my first. I just got to deliver a baby—a little girl—and I hope and pray that she'll never get shot by a robber. What is this world coming to? Out West, these people wear guns and the outlaws have in time gotten bad, really bad."

She didn't exactly know what to say to that. This man talked so fast she could hardly keep up with him. As if he didn't wait for a reply, he shoved his eyeglasses back up on his nose. With a glance down, he leaned forward and began to undo what the preacher had painstakingly wrapped around her shoulder.

"Now don't be afraid of anything. I just need to check and make sure that the pastor did a good job, though I'm almost positive he did. I wouldn't be doing my duty if I didn't check."

While he was talking, he began to inspect the open wound.

Ambrosia—well, Mrs. Mulberry—looked at Jarred and patted him on the arm. "While you were outside, your betrothed and I talked and I've invited her to come stay with me while she recuperates over the next week and then you two can get married. But I think this is best and during that time, you two can get to know each other a little bit better. How does that sound?"

Gabby stared at Mrs. Mulberry, shocked by her words. She fought not to groan as the doc checked her wound, sending a fresh shaft of pain through her.

The preacher looked in dismay at the older woman too. Behind him, Big John's shoulders shook as he chuckled.

"Now hold on, Mrs. Mulberry. I did not send for a bride. I'm sorry," he said to her then looked back at the smiling older woman. Gabby's head was spinning. "I was just going to ask you if you could provide a room for Miss Tyson while we sort through this and she

recuperates. I'm not sure what will need to be done."
He looked at her apologetically once more. "I'm very
sorry about all of this. I need some time to think about
it all and figure out what we should do for you. But
since I didn't write the letters and wasn't expecting a
wife to arrive, I hope you understand I'm not planning
on getting married."

Gabby nodded, unable to speak.

"Now, preacher. Let's not jump to conclusions.
This poor girl has been through a horrible, horrible
ordeal and we don't want to put her in shock or
anything learning this new bit of information. She'll be
at my house and you two can get to know each other
while we come up with a solution."

Compassion filled his eyes. He had very nice eyes.
She liked that compassion she saw in them.

"Very well, you're right, Mrs. Mulberry. Now is
not the time for this discussion. Thank you for inviting
her to stay at your home. That's very Christian of
you."

"Just trying to do the Lord's work. I've been
lonely in that house and well, you know my being here

is just like the good Lord put me where I was standing just so I can help out."

The preacher tugged his collar. Gabby almost felt sorry for him. Well, not almost—she *did* feel sorry for the poor man. He must be in a state of shock. But she had to admire the way that he was handling it. She didn't mind. Some men would've blown their stack.

"Well, if I get a vote on that," the doctor said, "I say that's a perfectly wonderful idea because despite the fact that you did an excellent job with her shoulder, I have to do some stitching and then it's going to need to be watched very carefully and doctored. We don't want infection to set in." He glanced at Mrs. Mulberry.

Mrs. Mulberry shook her head, looking very sad. "No, we do not want infection to set in. I will take very good care of you."

"I know you will, dear," the doc said. "But infection, as you know, can come out of the blue. We just need to make sure that that doesn't happen. I'll help you prepare. And I'll be by to check on her at least once a day. It will be nice knowing that she's in your hands, just in case that were to happen."

Gabby wondered what had happened in Mrs. Mulberry's life to make that sad look appear. *Did it have something to do with infection?*

Gabby wanted to know these things about the sweet lady. She remembered her saying her husband had passed away and it had been horrible. For the first time since Gabby had been shot, the realization hit her. She could have died and still could if the wound wasn't taken care of correctly. Gabby shuddered and thought about that bullet injury that she had gotten. *Surely, it would heal okay.* Surely, she didn't come all this way to die after getting shot by an outlaw. What a sad obituary that would be. And not the way she wanted her life to end.

She wanted to live, wanted to marry a man she loved, and completely understood she more than likely would not be marrying the preacher.

CHAPTER FOUR

It was quickly decided that she would go to Mrs. Mulberry's home and the very capable woman would take good care of her.

"Here, take a nice sip of this." The doctor handed her a little glass. She did as she was told and shivered as it went down.

Jarred and Big John eased her up; she felt a little woozy and swayed. The preacher— her reluctant groom—steadied her. Him being reluctant suddenly struck her as funny and she giggled and leaned into him.

"I promise, I won't make you marry me." She looked up into his handsome face. His face was kind of fuzzy and for a moment, there were two of them. Which was fine, because he was so handsome.

"Preacher, maybe you should carry her," the doctor said. "Since she's got a hold on you like that."

Her fingers tightened around his shirt and she realized she did have a hold on him. "Please do." She sighed and laid her head against his chest. His heart beat really fast against her ear and for a minute, she thought she went to sleep. The next thing she knew, they were in the buggy and it was moving down the street.

She squinted at the passing buildings through groggy eyes. "I don't know what that was that the doctor gave me, but I am feeling *noo* pain."

The buggy hit a bump and she fell against the preacher. "Yep, that lil-le sip of somethin' was powerful." She looked up and squinted at the two handsome preachers looking at her with horror. "You sure are nice to look at—even with your face all contorted like that."

She sighed and laid her hand on one of his faces. "It'll be okay. We'll get married, have a house full of kids and live happily ever after. Do you want kids?" She then leaned her head on his arm. She was so dizzy…and sleepy. Everything was blurry around the edges as she remembered he wasn't marrying her…or was he?

She patted Jarred's arm, so glad it wasn't Alfred's. Alfred…her daddy was probably really upset with her right now. But she just couldn't marry Alfred. She tried to focus on thinking about her daddy again, about whether he would come looking for her. She was pretty sure he would. But she was too tired to think about it. She sighed and then forgot everything as she snuggled against her groom and went to sleep.

Jarred barely caught Laura before she slid off the seat. He clutched her in his arms, not at all sure what to do.

Mrs. Mulberry smiled over the seat at him. "You are doing a great job with that sweet dear. Poor thing."

"Doc, what did you give her?"

The doctor chuckled. "Laudanum. It can be plumb entertaining the way it affects some folks. But she won't remember any of it. Including the pain of this buggy ride."

She was snoring in his arms and Jarred was quite certain she would not want to remember any of this. Including what she had been saying. She had called him handsome over and over again, and he could still feel the heat from her touch where she'd caressed his cheek.

The rain and the cattle drive through town had not helped the roads and so the doc had been pretty smart knocking her out like this. But he was highly uncomfortable with the situation.

He found her snoring a little endearing. If it had been like the bellowing of a cow, he might not have been so fond of it. But for now, it was cute. He bet she had no idea she snored. He decided he wanted to be the one to tell her.

They pulled up to Mrs. Mulberry's house and Jarred was in a predicament. Laura had snuggled against his shoulder and was snoring loudly. Mrs.

Mulberry was smiling and even the doc had a grin on his face.

Mrs. Mulberry hustled toward the front door. "Well, come on. That laudanum sure worked on her. Let's get her inside before it wears off."

Jarred wished someone else could do it, not feeling at all comfortable holding her close like this. But Big John hadn't thought he was needed, so he'd not squeezed into the buggy. That left it to him, considering the doc was old and smaller than any of them.

"Well, come on, Pastor," Mrs. Mulberry urged from the house.

Without any options, he maneuvered from the carriage and carried her up the walk and followed Mrs. Mulberry into the house and down the hall. Laura was light as he moved into the room where Mrs. Mulberry was pulling back covers. He felt uncomfortable as he placed her on the bed.

"How delightful that you are so strong, Pastor. Perfect for carrying her inside like this." The older woman beamed with what he thought was sheer delight.

"I'm glad I could help," he said, not exactly sure how to take her delight. "Mrs. Mulberry, I just want to make sure you understand that I did not send those letters and I'm not marrying Miss Tyson. I would appreciate it if you would not put false hope where there is none. Besides, it's easy to see we are not a suitable match, even if I could consider it."

She frowned across the bed at him. "Hogwash. How can you tell such a thing in the short while that you've known her? Not suitable indeed. She'll recuperate and we shall take our time on everything else."

He stared down at the sleeping beauty and his heart tugged. Thankfully, the doctor entered the room and Jarred backed toward the door as the doctor checked her pulse. "I'll wait out here for you, Doctor." He made it out of the room but couldn't help looking back over his shoulder for one more glance at the peacefully snoring young woman.

The woman who'd come to marry him.

"As a matter of fact, I'll walk back to the church."

He headed out into the fresh air, strode out the gate and down the rutted road. He needed time to think. And to thank the Lord for sparing Miss Tyson's life. That bullet could have easily killed her.

Her sweet smile filled his mind and suddenly he knew he also needed time to pray as he dug his hands into his pockets and headed toward the church.

CHAPTER FIVE

By the second day she had arrived, Gabby felt better. Mrs. Mulberry had taken very good care of her and was excellent with wound care. The doctor had come by that morning; he checked her and the wound, and said it was healing nicely and that her color was looking better. Her body was rebuilding the blood that she had lost in her ordeal and her energy level was returning. She had had time to sit around and recuperate. One of Mrs. Mulberry's friends had come over with chicken noodle soup. The sweet, bird-like lady had insisted she call her Miss Essie Jane and not

Mrs. Tate. The sweet lady had washed her hair for her, using a pail of water and scented soap.

Gabby was glad that the doctor had said she was strong enough to have a bath today. She still had very little energy, though, but would find the energy to bathe the dirt off her after riding on that stagecoach. With Mrs. Mulberry's help, she accomplished getting in and out of the tub and then dressed. Now she sat in the front room, feeling the best she'd felt since before the confrontation with the robber.

"Okay, my dear, I've brought you some scones. And some tea. This will make you feel much better." She set the dish on the side table just as there was a knock on the front door. "Oh, I'll be right back."

Gabby took a bite of the cherry scone and it practically melted in her mouth it was so delightful and delicious. Gabby decided that before she left, she would have to convince Mrs. Mulberry to teach her how to make these.

"That was our sweet pastor come to check on you. But I told him to come back tomorrow when you would feel a little bit better."

Gabby was relieved. She still felt so weak and uncertain. *What was she going to do?* The poor man hadn't sent for her and so this was really awkward. "Thank you. I feel so awful."

"Why, it's not your fault that someone pretended to be him and sent for a bride. Besides, I think it's a very good idea. He needs a bride. Essie Jane agrees. He is a wonderful pastor and man. And some lucky woman is going to get him. Why not you? If we had more single women around here, they would all be vying for his attention. He is one of our most eligible bachelors."

"But—"

The mischievous gleam in her eye halted Gabby's words.

"Me and Essie Jane have been talking and we think that we might jump on the bandwagon and help the mystery cupid out. That's what we call whoever sent for you. We've decided you should fight for your man."

Shocked, Gabby blinked and her stomach quivered with unease. The weight on her shoulders from the lies she'd been telling were eating at her soul. "I have something to confess," she said.

Mrs. Mulberry's eyes widened. "Oh, you look distressed. What is it, dear? What do you need to confess?"

Gabby took a deep breath. "I'm not who I'm saying that I am. I'm not Laura Tyson. I'm Gabby Anson. Laura was our maid back in St. Louis. She wrote the letters to the pastor—I mean, to the person pretending to be him. I took her place when she got cold feet and backed out."

Mrs. Mulberry looked shocked but recovered quickly as she contemplated her words. "So your name is Gabby?"

She nodded. "Yes, and you see my dilemma. I've lied to get here. The pastor deserves better than a liar like me. Besides, I had planned to start a small business or something when I arrived in town and not to hold the pastor to his promise. I was just using it as an escape from my situation. I had money until the hold-up."

"And what was your situation?"

"I had consented to marry a very nice young man. And…well, with every passing moment that the wedding neared, I grew leery and less and less inclined to go through with the wedding. So the night before my wedding, when Laura confessed her situation and that she could not go through with becoming a mail-order bride, I asked her if I could take her place. She gave me the letters. Because she had cold feet, she understood what I was feeling. I became a runaway bride and now a mail-order bride with no options since the robber stole my money. I know no one, have no money and no way to open a business. And I can't force the pastor to do something he didn't agree to in the first place. I'm in a dire predicament. I may have to send a letter to my father and ask if he would help me come back home."

Mrs. Mulberry was lost in thought. "Don't jump to conclusions that quickly. I was talking to Big John yesterday and he said the good Lord works in mysterious ways and I agree. I think that we should give this a chance and let Him work this out. Yes, you've done right in confessing and now you can start fresh. And let the Lord work fresh. I can promise you that Pastor Andrews will not judge you. At least, now that you've come clean and expressed your situation."

Gabby wasn't sure whether to feel relieved or not. But at least she didn't have to feel guilty any longer and that was good.

She would confess to Jarred and see where it went. That was the only option she had...

Jarred had been feeling restless since he'd left Laura at Mrs. Mulberry's. He had gone each day to get a report on how she was doing. It was his Christian duty and as pastor of the small town, he liked checking on people when they were sick or down and trying to help them in any way that he could. But after three days of Mrs. Mulberry giving him a report but not inviting him in to see Laura, he was beginning to feel disgruntled. He wanted to see her.

It was true. He found himself thinking about her as the days had passed. She'd braved traveling the wilderness on her own to come to an uncertain future and that had to be admired. Thinking of her snores on his shoulder made him chuckle several times since he'd dropped her off. But he stopped smiling when he thought about the fact that she'd been in a terrible situation, being robbed, and she hadn't whined about it. She'd been worried most by the fact that her purse had been stolen. That had been because any money she had owned had been in that bag. He could only imagine how she must feel now, having nothing. He thought she was handling it bravely. He admired that.

Today, Mrs. Mulberry had said she was allowing visitors. The widow had surprised him with her guarding of her patient. She had been resolute in her opinion that Laura needed her rest and time to build up some energy before having visitors…including him.

Now, as he walked up to the front porch of her home, he felt a sense of anticipation at seeing the woman who'd come here thinking she was going to be his wife.

That was a strange thought. It seemed awkward

but yet it wasn't completely off-putting to him as he knocked lightly on the front door.

Mrs. Mulberry opened the door with a huge smile. "Pastor Andrews, so glad to have you. Come in, come in."

He stepped inside. Though he was used to her exuberant personality, today she seemed especially excited.

"Pastor Andrews, come in, come in. Isn't it a beautiful day today?"

He smiled, a bit startled by her welcome. "Thank you. I hope you and Miss Tyson are doing well today."

"We are. The good Lord's been good to me. And Ga—Laura is much better. Right this way. She's sitting in the parlor."

He caught the stumble over Laura's name and wondered about that as he followed her into the front parlor. He stopped in the doorway, startled, when he saw Laura sitting there, looking like a beautiful angel. Her skin was still pale but her cheeks had pink to them and there was a brightness to her eyes as she smiled at him. Despite everything, he was spellbound. Something about her took his breath away. Her hair gleamed and was pulled back in a casual, soft bun that left wisps trailing about her face. And she wore a pretty pink dress that fit loose at the top, which was probably due to something they'd done to it to make room for her injury. She had a light shawl wrapped around her shoulders. It made him think that for practical purposes, they probably hadn't buttoned her dress up all the way in the back because of her wounded shoulder inside the dress. His practical mind was thinking these things. Or maybe his brain wasn't thinking because he was at a loss for words.

"Hello, Pastor." Her words faltered on *pastor*, as if she didn't know exactly what to call him.

"Please, call me Jarred."

She looked down her hands fidgeting on a handkerchief that she was holding. "I'm not sure that's appropriate." She looked troubled and glanced at Mrs. Mulberry.

The older lady nodded at her. "I'm going to

excuse myself and give you two some time to discuss things. I'll bring some tea in just a second, okay?" She backed out the door and was gone.

"Please, have a seat." Laura softly motioned to the chair.

He took a seat and tried to form words. His heart thumped and he couldn't look away from her. *What was wrong with him?* Finally, he managed to get his mind to work. "You look like you feel better," he said.

She clasped her hands together and fidgeted. "I feel much better but I need to talk to you."

"What can I do for you?"

"I just need to explain some things. First, I'm not who you think I am. I was supposed to get married five days ago and I said I couldn't do it and so my maid was supposed to get married also, only she was supposed to be a mail-order bride and come here to marry you but she got cold feet and backed out. And I backed out of my marriage and took her place to come here and start a new life."

"You aren't Laura Tyson?"

"No, I'm Gabby Anson." She closed her eyes

momentarily. "I thought it best to be truthful as soon as possible. I'd like to start over, being truthful. I was supposed to get married but got cold feet and knew I couldn't go through with it. Alfred was very nice but not for me. My maid Laura confessed to me that she was supposed to be leaving on the train the next morning to catch a stagecoach as a mail-order bride but she couldn't go through with it. I took her ticket because I couldn't go through with my wedding either." She explained her situation a bit more calmly than her first outburst.

"So I couldn't pass the opportunity up for a new start. I gathered up some of my things and a little money and became a runaway bride. And here I am, only I wasn't expecting to get robbed. I'm sorry. I planned to tell you the truth when I got here and to tell you that she was so sorry she couldn't go through with it. And then I planned to start a business of some sort but now I have no money and am not sure what I'm going to do. But you can rest easy and not have to worry about any of that. I've thought about it since I confessed to Mrs. Mulberry, and I think my only recourse is to send a letter to my father and ask him if he could send me the money to get me back home where I can face up to what I've done. I can try to mend fences and you can go about your business as usual."

He was dumbfounded. "Thank you for being honest. I appreciate it." He tried to process what she'd revealed. Everything since she had arrived had thrown him completely off balance, from finding out that she was supposed to marry him to now learning that she wasn't who she said she was and that she wasn't supposed to marry him. And that she was going to leave. He didn't owe her anything and she didn't owe him anything. And that meant she didn't have anything holding her here, so there was no reason for her to stay. *So why did he feel so terrible right now?*

Though it had been a shock when he'd learned she'd come here as his mail-order bride, he'd been anticipating the last couple of days when Mrs. Mulberry would let him see her again. He'd been exploring the idea of getting to know her.

And now she was leaving.

"I'm really sorry," she said after a moment, searching his gaze.

"I'm sure that your parents and your fiancé are very worried about you. And the rest of your family."

"I'm sure they are. I have three sisters and I would be terribly worried about them. But Alfred will have to get over it because even if I go back, I will not be marrying him."

"If you feel that way, why did you agree to marry him in the first place?"

"It is just that he was a business acquaintance of my father's and it was a good match. My parents were both very in favor of it. So I agreed. Then I started dreaming of adventure and seeing something other than St. Louis and I felt smothered."

"I see. But you didn't talk to Alfred about this at all? You just left?"

"I know, it was not the best way. I panicked. It is all my fault. I agree. But I can't take it back. And now I'm shot, stranded, and have put you in an awkward spot."

He shook his head. "Nothing that can't be fixed

has happened, except if you had been fatally shot. That would have been a tragedy. I don't see why you would have to leave so quickly. You're not in the shape to leave this moment, I wouldn't think. Your shoulder's not recuperated enough. And Mrs. Mulberry has already said you are welcome to stay here, so there is no rush for you to leave. Just between you and me, she's probably enjoying your being here. Why don't we all discuss that when she returns with the tea and scones?"

He felt better about being able to put his being a pastor into the mix. This was about what was going on in Gabby's life to have her take such a drastic measure to get away from St. Louis. He wanted to make sure she had time to think about what was best. For her.

Solving problems was part of his job description. He liked helping. And in this instance, he wanted to buy her some time to get her life in order. Was he also buying himself a little bit of time? *Maybe.*

He wanted to get to know her better without the mail-order bride situation hanging over their head.

"If Mrs. Mulberry is agreeable, then thank you. I

think what you're suggesting is the perfect thing for right now and then, when I'm better, then I will go."

He liked that she wasn't leaving, at least not yet. "Good, I'm glad…Gabby. And I like your name. It fits you."

"Thank you."

Mrs. Mulberry came into the room at that time, all smiles as she carried a tray with tea and scones on it.

His stomach growled, just thinking about the scones.

CHAPTER SIX

"I totally agree," Mrs. Mulberry said the instant she heard the plan. "I insist that you stay as long as you like."

"Only if you're sure," Gabby said.

Mrs. Mulberry looked shocked. "Of course I am. I'm enjoying having you here. There's so many things we can do. We can have a church social—now, we love to have those—and well, maybe Pastor Andrews can show you around the country a little bit. It is beautiful country." She smiled at Pastor Andrews.

"I'd love to." He smiled and she thought he truly

looked as if he wanted to show her around. That made Gabby feel better. He had just been staring at her blankly for a moment when she'd been explaining what she'd done. It had worried her but she knew it was a lot to take in. It had worried her so much.

Now her heartbeat scrambled inside her chest at the thought of spending time with him.

Gabby reminded herself that she was not cut out to be a pastor's wife and letting herself get all flustered about him was not a good idea. But she couldn't stop what her heart was doing. He was nice and he was handsome and appealing and despite the warning going off in her brain, she found herself nodding. "Okay, I'd love that too."

He rose. "Then I'm going to leave now and let you rest. I'll come back tomorrow around this time and we'll go on a ride." His smile warmed her all over.

And she found herself looking forward to their ride more than anything she'd looked forward to in a very long time.

As he was leaving, the sheriff arrived to ask her a few questions and with him was his wife.

"You have more company, Gabby." Mrs. Mulberry led them into the front parlor. "This is Sheriff Trey Jones and his wife, Lucy. We are so excited Lucy is here. She was our first mail-order bride."

Lucy smiled warmly. "It's true." She chuckled and held her hand out. "I'm Lucy and I'm so glad I came here." She looked at Trey. There was pure love in her eyes as the two looked at each other.

"Not any happier than I am that you're here," the sheriff said.

Gabby felt her heart tug and realized that that was something she wanted and one of the main reasons she hadn't been able to go through with marrying Alfred. Although she thought Alfred was a nice man, there just had not been anything there in her heart that would resemble love at all. They had barely even kissed; it had been a small peck on the lips that had inspired nothing. And the thought of marrying someone she had no feelings for—the romantic kind—just ate at her. And so here she sat now, seeing that genuine love sparking between these two. It gave her the assurance that she wanted that and she would not, if she returned home, be even considering marrying Alfred again, even if he offered. Which she doubted he would. No, she would hold out for love.

If she could afford to. And that was the problem.

She wanted to have the courage to be independent and take her destiny into her own hands. "I'm glad I came, even if I end up having to go back. I'm glad that it worked out good for you. I'm not thrilled about being robbed but it's a risk that comes with coming out West."

"That's true," Sheriff Jones said. "But I'm still sorry it happened to you and I've come to ask you a few questions. Lucy came to offer you moral support. Do you feel like answering a few questions about your ordeal?"

"Anything I can help you with, I'd be happy to. I'm not sure what I can tell you."

"Can you describe the man? Did he have anything that would help us identify him?"

She would never forget him. "He was medium height and though he had a cowboy hat on, he had brown hair. He wore a bandana and his hair was unkempt, shaggy around his collar. Oh, and his shirt was a brown color too."

"Is there any detail about him that might be unusual? Anything that might give us more to go on? Think really hard."

She thought hard, trying to think of something. "It was pretty traumatic and I'm having a hard time thinking about that. I can't think of anything right now."

She felt terrible that she couldn't tell him anything better.

"It's okay. Maybe while you're here, you'll remember something else. It's a good thing you'll be around for at least a little while."

"The robber took my money, so I have nothing. I had hoped that maybe I could come out here and maybe open a small business of some sort."

"Would you want a job?" Lucy asked.

Gabby nodded. "Yes, I would consider taking a job. I'm going to be staying here with Mrs. Mulberry. It may take me a few days to get all of my strength back but as soon as I am able, I would love to find a job."

"We will have to see what we can come up with," Mrs. Mulberry said. She and Lucy looked at each other, as if conspiring.

Gabby could tell that their minds were working as they tried to figure out something that she could do for a job.

Lucy smiled again. "The town has some things that we're lacking and you being here might give us an opportunity to come up with something that could help add to the town."

"Oh, that is a certainty," the older woman said, smiling a huge smile.

Gabby hoped so.

CHAPTER SEVEN

The next day, despite being determined not to be nervous, she was as she waited on the front porch swing for Jarred to arrive. She was feeling better physically, but still not herself. Her energy remained low and her shoulder still hurt but, thankfully, not like it had. She was able to button the back of her dress, which made her happy. Progress was being made.

"I just know you're going to have a great time today. Fresh air will do you some good." Mrs. Mulberry fussed about her, fluffing her pillow after she sat a glass of water beside her. "And the company of your young man."

Gabby started to remind the older woman that he was not her young man but didn't waste her breath. What good would it do? Instead, she smiled and took a sip of the water.

Jarred pulled into view down the street and her pulse kicked up a notch at the sight of him sitting tall in the seat of a carriage.

"Oh, there he is." Mrs. Mulberry sighed. "Such a handsome man, don't you think?"

Gabby smiled at that. "Yes, he is." There was no denying it, so she didn't try.

He hopped from the carriage and strode quickly up the walk. "Ladies, good afternoon." He stepped onto the porch and swept his cowboy hat from his head. "You look like you're feeling better today, Gabby."

Her cheeks heated as his gaze swept from Mrs. Mulberry and landed on her. "I am. And I am so thankful to be going for a ride."

"And she's ready for some fresh air," Mrs. Mulberry added. "I'll be right back. You go ahead and get her to the buggy, preacher." Mrs. Mulberry disappeared inside the house, leaving them alone.

"What would you like to see first?"

"I'm anxious to see the town. I was out both times that I went through town." She frowned. "Whatever the doctor gave me for pain wiped me out for the ride to Mrs. Mulberry's."

His eyes twinkled. "Yes, you were out for both. I have to say on the ride here you had your head on my shoulder and you were definitely out cold." He held his hand out. "Let me help you up. And then let me know how I need to assist you."

She took his hand and tingles of awareness spiked up her arm as butterflies frolicked in her chest. Her mouth went dry. "This is fine. I'm much stronger. If you'll just give me your arm as we walk down the path." She stood and was glad she didn't wobble, because her knees had gone weak just seeing him. *What was the matter with her?* It wasn't as if she hadn't ever been around a handsome man before. But it was him. Something about Jarred was different. He affected her like no one else ever had.

Concern etched his expression. "Whatever you

need." He held his arm for her to take and she linked hers through his. They started walking and he placed his free hand over her arm, as if to secure her further. It was very comforting. They walked down the path and when they reached the buggy, he assisted her as she stepped on the step and then into the carriage.

"This is much easier than one of the wagons would have been."

"I rented it from the livery because I thought it might work better for you."

His consideration touched her. "Thank you. You've gone to a lot of trouble—"

"It's no trouble at all. I'm benefiting from it with your company." She was on eye level with him and her heart caught as his eyes warmed. "I mean that, Gabby. I've been looking forward to our ride."

Oh, the butterflies were dancing in her chest. "Me too," she managed.

"Here you go," Mrs. Mulberry called as she hurried from the house and down the walk. She carried a medium-sized basket. "I've packed a picnic lunch for you two to enjoy. And here is a blanket to spread on the ground." She held her arm out and offered the basket to Jarred. He looked startled as he took the basket and then the blanket she held in her other arm.

"Thank you, Mrs. Mulberry. That's very thoughtful of you."

She blushed. "Oh, it's nothing. I just want you two to have fun and I didn't want Gabby to get too tired," she said directly to Jarred. "I thought a rest would do her good after you show her the countryside."

"Thank you. That's very kind of you." Gabby couldn't help but be pleasantly surprised by the actions of her new friend. The thought of the picnic with Jarred was exciting. She wasn't cut out to be a preacher's wife but she wasn't going to dwell on that right now; she was too ready to get out of the house and he was too nice.

He climbed in beside her. "Main Street coming up and then onward to the countryside. How does that sound?"

"That sounds good." The idea of seeing the countryside with him was most appealing.

They waved to the smiling Mrs. Mulberry and then headed down the street. The town was a combination of rustic and quaint. There was a diner, a mercantile, a feed store. The big man she remembered from the first day was carrying some feed to a wagon and he smiled and waved.

"I'm glad you're feeling better," he called as Jarred slowed and halted beside him. "You gave us a mighty big scare."

"Thank you. I want to thank you for all you did. I was told you helped get the doctor."

"No thanks needed. I was just helping out and glad to assist. Looks like you're getting the tour."

She smiled brightly. "I am. I'm ready to see everything and getting out of the house feels great."

"Good. Good. I'll let you get on your way." He stepped back. "You take good care of her, preacher."

Jarred chuckled. "Oh, you can be assured of that."

They were moving again. Moments later, they spotted Lucy Jones and a little girl coming down the street. She waved and Jarred again stopped the buggy.

"Good afternoon," Lucy called and, holding the cute little girl's hand, they walked over to the buggy. "I'm so glad to see you out and about. This is my daughter Janie."

"I heard you got shot," Janie said, her eyes wide. "I'm glad you're all better."

"Thank you. I'm better thanks to everyone who helped me."

"Good. My daddy went looking for the robber. He'll get him."

Alarm filled Gabby thinking about this child's daddy out there in danger, looking for the gunman who'd shot her.

"Don't worry," Lucy said, as if reading her mind. "Trey knows how to take care of himself. And there is a posse with him."

"He should be home soon," Jarred added. "It's not your fault that a robber held up the stage, Gabby. You don't need to take that burden. The sheriff would have had to go out looking for him whether you'd been shot or not."

"That's right," Lucy agreed. "And Trey is very good and very careful."

She took a deep breath and tried not to feel responsible. They were right. It wasn't her fault, but if anything happened to him she would feel to blame. She prayed he would be okay.

CHAPTER EIGHT

They made it to the outskirts of town after leaving Lucy and Janie. She tried hard not to worry and began to enjoy the ride. Jarred had explained the different shops and who owned them. He talked about the people who lived in town and she really got the sense that he truly cared for each family and worried about those who were sick and in need. He truly had a heart for people.

"The town really is in need of more females. We need families but there are no women to become brides. I'm afraid if we don't find a way to bring in more ladies here, the town will start to dwindle. But it will take women with adventurous spirits to come. Sadly, many who came a few years ago when travel was still so hard haven't made it. I worry about my town. And the men." He tugged on the reins of the buggy and turned the horse toward the countryside.

He glanced at her. "It gets lonely here. I know for myself, it is busy as I am tending to my people. But I get lonesome. I would love to have a wife. I keep saying that I'm waiting for the Lord to send me the right woman. To be honest, I began to think that that might not happen and well, I've been thinking about you. I can't help but be surprised that you're here. And after your story, I understand a bit better. It explains the whole thing a lot better. I have to admit that you intrigued me."

Her pulse raced as if the buggy was flying across the countryside. "I must confess to you that I can't imagine myself married to a preacher. Especially after what I've done. The fact that I lied like I did would probably be a terrible thing for you to overlook. But even if you could, I don't think I have what it would take."

He slowed the horse to a halt and stared at her, concern on his face. "Why would you say that? You're in a tight spot and you did something you felt you needed to do. I'm not holding anything against you. I can understand your worrying in some respects because leading the flock can sometimes be hard. Sometimes life is not your own. You minister to the sick and bring joy and comfort to them when they're sad or grieving. Sometimes it's hard on a person. I don't see why you don't think you could do that."

She bit her lip. "Not that we're talking about me and you. That's no longer a thing. I'm just saying you need someone who is right for the position."

"I believe you don't give yourself enough credit. But I sometimes think my burden would be hard on the wife. I can see why you would worry but not because you're not worthy."

They stared at each other for a long moment and she had the strongest need to help him in his ministry. It scared her. His burden touched her heart. Jarred was such a good man.

And he was not judging her but instead building her up. Suddenly she realized that if he wasn't a preacher, there would be nothing standing in her way of wanting to be his wife.

They hadn't known each other very long at all but unlike how she felt about Alfred, she knew something told her, deep in her heart, that she could love Jarred.

The very idea had her stiffening.

"Are you okay?" His beautiful eyes filled with concern. "Are you in pain?"

"No, I'm not. I, I just thought of something in…" Her voice trailed off as she realized she couldn't tell him what she just thought about. "Do you think maybe we could find that picnic spot? I am getting a little bit hungry. And I'm anxious to see if maybe Mrs. Mulberry included some of those scones of hers. I have to admit that my waistline might increase if I stay at her house too long."

"Okay, sure." He then winked. "I have to admit I worry about the same thing. She brings in a box of those every week and my mouth waters just thinking about them. There are a lot of fellas who would fight me over a box of her scones. We agree on that but not your heart. You have a good heart."

She blushed. "Okay, thank you. She's told me that as soon as I'm able, she's going to teach me how to make them."

His eyes got dreamy and it did something to her pulse. "Well, I have to say that if you could make scones like Mrs. Mulberry, you would be my dream woman." He chuckled. "I definitely have a weakness."

She suddenly had the oddest need to learn how to make scones. And that in itself was shocking because baking had never been something that appealed to her.

Jarred was drawn to Gabby and thought she was wonderful. She had listened with interest and deep compassion in her eyes as he'd talked about his ministry. She might not think she had it and he didn't understand that but he saw the worry in her eyes for those he talked about and for the sheriff when she'd learned he was out looking for the robber. She was a good woman.

They had known each other such a short time but he felt as if he had known her for a long time. And when she looked at him and her eyes warmed, it did something to his heart.

And it had nothing to do with the scones.

Of course, if she learned how to make the scones, it was true she would be his dream girl. But something about Gabby seemed to call out to him. He had thought about her all night. He sat on the porch last night but it had been lonely to sit there as he thought about her. And now he was concerned about the fact that she could leave.

He drove the buggy over toward a small clearing by the brook that ran alongside the road not too far away. It was the perfect spot for a picnic. They would eat and then he would take her on a little bit farther drive. But this was a beautiful spot. Mrs. Mulberry had thought of everything. He took the basket and the blanket out of the wagon and helped Gabby out of the buggy. They walked over near the clearing. He spread the blanket out and then helped her get settled on the blanket.

"Is your shoulder feeling okay?" he asked after she was sitting.

"I'm fine. It still hurts some but I'm enjoying this outing so much I'm hardly feeling it."

He sat down beside her. "I'm enjoying it too but the minute you're ready to head back, just let me know." He opened the basket and lifted out a plate of fresh cherry scones. He grinned. "We have a treasure. I don't even think we need to look farther in the basket but knowing Mrs. Mulberry, there something else in there that's wonderful."

"I agree. So far, everything I've ever had has been wonderful. I'm not the best cook. I have to confess that I'm looking forward to learning how to make some of the things she does."

He wasn't worried about cooking skills. If she could make the scones, that would be a plus, but he lived off most of his own cooking for a long time; he lived this long—he could live longer on it. He was interested in a wife who was pleasant and loving and who could love him and he could love.

"Oh," Gabby exclaimed. "She made chicken

salad. And fresh bread."

"She makes the best," he said. Next, they pulled out jars of water. And a few other things to go along with it. "I think we're going to owe her a big thank-you when we get back to town."

"I agree." She reached for a scone, smiled then bit into the sweet, delightful dessert. He laughed and picked one up too.

"Dessert first." He chuckled and took a bite.

"We're bad." She then took another bite.

"It's our meal—we can eat it as we choose."

"You are a man after my own heart."

He watched her take a bite of scone and found himself wishing what she said was true and he could be the man of her heart.

After they'd eaten for a little while, enjoying the breeze in the pretty afternoon and the gurgling of the brook beside them, Gabby relaxed and it seemed that Jarred did also. They had both been thrown into this situation and it wasn't quite like what they thought it would be. They were at a crossroads concerning where they would go from here but she realized that she liked him, whether he was a pastor or not—whether she was pastor wife material or not. They laughed; they enjoyed the scones and it was nice.

"What made you become a preacher?" she asked after a little while, finding that she was very curious about him. He had a kind spirit and it was easy to see it in his eyes. But there was also a strength about him that was undeniable. He wasn't a small man; he was very fit, very much so, and she couldn't help but notice that. His arms had muscles, well-toned muscles, that had the look of a man who knew how to split wood and work for a living, not just stand behind a pulpit and preach to people. She had a feeling that he did things that were active like that.

He took a sip of his water and looked from her to the babbling brook. His expression was thoughtful. The lines between his eyes crinkled as she was pulled toward him, wondering what brought the seriousness there. When he looked back at her, he gave her a small smile.

"I had a rough upbringing. I was orphaned early. I spent a lot of time in Northridge—that's my parents where died—but before that, I was on the street and it was rough. I got into trouble." He shrugged. "Got in with the wrong crowd. But when you're on the street, near hungry, in Philadelphia, it's hard not to get into trouble. But I was gathered up and taken to an orphanage. Life there wasn't rosy but I got three meals a day and had a small cot with a blanket to sleep with, so I was grateful. There was a nun there who was kind and the lady who ran the place was kind. I've heard stories of some orphanages where that wasn't the case, but I got lucky. When the younger kids were sick or they needed something, I helped out and found that I like helping out. Maybe because, growing up, I didn't have anyone to rely on, I found comforting the younger kids who were in the orphanage rewarding. But I didn't know the Lord. When the war came along, I was of the age that I was leaving the orphanage and was pulled into the war. And I ended up being pulled into helping on the medical end. I got wounded pretty quickly into it and was sent to the infirmary. That's where I learned to care for wounds. And why I was able to help you."

"And I'm grateful. So grateful. As I'm sure all those you helped during the war were grateful."

"I hope I was able to be a blessing. There was so much pain and suffering and it was during my time there that a chaplain led me to the Lord. And that helped me to be able to give comfort to the men, even those who were dying."

"I'm sure you were a great comfort."

She suddenly wondered who comforted him. She could hear the pain in his voice. He'd seen so much and it hurt him.

"When the war was over, I came West. I had nothing to hold me anywhere and I needed the open space. I'd heard that Texas was the land of opportunity. I came this way and it just seemed natural—I took on the role of a pastor. When I came here, there was no pastor and along the way, a lot of the places that I stopped in there were no churches. When I arrived here, there was a church building but there was no pastor. They had a circuit pastor, which is kind of what I was doing. As I traveled, I would preach where needed, offer comfort but I didn't stay. I was drawn to come to finish my travel to Texas. And I ended up here."

She was mesmerized by him. Her heart ached that he had had it so hard. And though he was happy and saw joy in giving comfort to everyone, she found that she longed to give him comfort. She suddenly longed to wrap her arms around him and hold him close. It was powerful. The most powerful thing she ever felt. It nearly brought tears to her eyes. She blinked hard and looked away from him, overwhelmed by emotion.

His hand startled her as his thumb brushed on her cheek. She realized that he was brushing a tear away.

"You're crying," he said softly. "Why are you crying?"

His hand was so gentle and she found herself rubbing her cheek against his hand as she turned to look at him, to meet his gaze. Her heart thundered.

"I was so touched by your story." She hesitated, and then reached up and touched his cheek. She couldn't help herself. She wanted so much to offer him comfort. And she had never taken such liberty before. "I can't help wonder why no one has found you yet."

They stared at each other. Her heart thundered and then he leaned forward and gently, ever so gently, he kissed her. It was touching and filled her like the sun rising in the morning. He pulled away and looked into her eyes. And she felt that she would die if he didn't kiss her again. He looked as dazed as she felt and then to her relief and her joy, he kissed her again. His arms wrapped gently around her, so careful not to harm her shoulder as he drew her close. And he deepened the kiss. Her hand went to his heart—it pounded just like hers—and the strength of his lips intensified. Suddenly, he pulled away.

"I'm sorry," he rasped. "I didn't mean to do that but you are so lovely and I, to be honest, I've never felt drawn to anyone like you."

"I feel the same way." They stayed that way for the longest time, him holding her, no words.

And she could have stayed that way forever.

What was wrong with her? Whatever it was, it was magical.

Finally, he pulled away and cupped her face between his hands and brushed her lips gently again with his.

He smiled. "It seems that we have a dilemma."

"A dilemma?" Her heart still raced and joy radiated throughout her. There was teasing in his eyes and she realized that he had a teasing spirit—gentle and caring and teasing. It was a strong and potent combination.

"I think that I like kissing you and holding you even more than I like Mrs. Mulberry's scones. What am I going to do?"

She laughed. "Well, if it's any consolation, I feel the same." A blush heated her cheeks.

"I think maybe, if you don't mind—if you're in agreement—that I might come and sit on the porch with you a few nights at Mrs. Mulberry's."

"I would like that." She wasn't sure what she was saying or what she was doing. She wasn't cut out to be a preacher's wife but she found that she couldn't say no to seeing him again. It was impossible to say no when you wanted something so badly.

"Well, I guess for propriety's sake, I better take you back. Though, to be quite honest, it might be the very toughest thing I've ever done in my life." He smiled at her and the teasing in his eyes was replaced with seriousness.

She understood him completely. He helped her up, pulled her into his arms and held her once more. He kissed the top of her head and then let her go. She wished he would kiss her again. Instead, he gathered the blanket and the picnic basket and put it in the buggy and helped her up into the seat. And then they were off on the drive back.

CHAPTER NINE

When they arrived home, he took her hand and helped her from the carriage. Warmth spread up her arm and through her body. Something magical had happened on that simple ride with Jarred. Something in her heart had clicked into place and though she wasn't completely sure she understood it, she knew her life was forever changed. Could she so simply, so quickly, so absolutely have fallen—or at least begun to fall—in love with Jarred?

After leaving Gabby at Mrs. Mulberry's house, Jarred drove slowly back toward the livery to return the carriage. He felt dazed, stunned really. He had been unable to stop himself from kissing Gabby. He had told her his story, something he had never told anyone. No one. No one but the Lord knew what he had been through in his life. But he had told Gabby, sitting there on that bank of that brook. Normally if someone by chance had asked him about his life, he would change the subject and ask about them rather than talk about himself. It usually worked but with Gabby, he had felt genuine, heartfelt interest. And, after all, he was drawn to her already; he just hadn't completely realized how much. And he opened his heart to her, had told her about his life growing up, about the war, the pain. He let her glimpse inside his heart to dark places that he usually wished to leave alone. The Lord knew, and that was enough, he told himself. But he was deceiving himself because he knew on dark, lonely nights that it was those secrets, that pain, that had kept him isolated.

He led a life surrounded by people, reaching out trying to help people, and yet he remained locked inside himself. It was in essence a prison of his own making. But with Gabby, he released it, had told her exactly how he felt and she had cried.

His gut had wrenched and his heart had ached when he had seen the tear roll from the corner of her beautiful eyes, down the gentle slope of her cheek. Capturing that tear had been like touching her heart. It had conveyed so much emotion. And when she turned and looked at him, so much more emotion showed in her bright eyes. And he had kissed her.

Drawn to her like the ocean to the shore, he had been unable to stop himself, had no desire to stop himself. He wanted her so desperately in his arms and he knew that right now, there was nothing he wanted more than to have Gabby in his life forever. He barely knew her but he knew how he felt.

And the possibility that she might leave tore him up. She'd had so many shocking events happen since her arrival: being robbed, being shot, being told that the man she had come all this way to marry wasn't expecting her—despite the fact that he knew she wasn't the real bride who'd written the letters, that was still a shock.

He felt like maybe in her heart she now wished

she had written the letters. At least he prayed she felt that way. Because he wished with all of his heart that he had written those letters to her.

He spotted Big John standing outside his feed store. He pulled the buggy to a halt when Big John waved for him to stop.

"How's it going, preacher? How was your ride with the pretty Miss Tyson? You two look like you were having a mighty fine morning."

Big John was well respected and offered good advice. And Jarred knew this. Maybe that was why, in the next sentence, he opened up.

"In all honesty, Big John, I'm a little dazed right now. I had a wonderful afternoon. Probably the most wonderful afternoon of my life."

The feed store owner crossed his arms and grinned a smile as large as he was. He was known for his large heart and wise words. Right now, his smile was reassuring to Jarred.

"Well, I think that's mighty wonderful. You know that sweet girl put a lot of trust in coming here."

"Well, everyone's going to know it soon. And you

should probably be one of the first to know but actually her name isn't Laura Tyson. Her name is Gabby Anson. And she is basically a runaway bride. She told me all this yesterday after she confessed the truth to Mrs. Mulberry."

He related the story quickly and watched John's expression. There was no judgment there. But the man's forehead wrinkled and he rubbed his chin slowly with his fingers.

"So she's not who she says she was but, yet she came here anyway. And all this happened to her. And now she may be going home?"

"That's correct."

"And how you feel about that? Do you want her to go?"

He frowned and his shoulders drooped. "Honestly, I don't. That's why I'm so dazed right now. I wish I had been the one to write the letters to her. I wish I had been the one corresponding with her and that she was the one who had chosen to come out here to marry me. How can I feel this in such a short amount of time?"

Big John's smile grew even bigger. "When I fell

for my sweetie, I knew almost immediately that she was the one for me. We didn't have a big romance or a long, drawn-out engagement. She knew it and I knew it. I had gone to visit my uncle and met her at a church function. We were both at the punch bowl and started talking and then found a swing and we sat down and kept talking. I knew before I left that night that she was the one for me. I didn't leave from visiting my uncle until she agreed to marry me. That took only three days. And we were married all those years until I lost her. I would give anything for those years. And to think—I just went to visit my uncle. It's funny how happenstance can happen. I truly do believe that the Lord works in mysterious ways and when it's meant to be, it is meant to be. He will direct your paths to the right person. You're a man of the cloth—do you agree?"

Jarred let Big John's words wrap around him and his heart lightened. "Well, sir, this morning you have taken me to church. I do agree with you. But, you know, sometimes a man can let too much thought get in the way of his heart. I need to pray and listen to what the Lord is pressing upon me. Thank you. I do wonder who was pretending to be me and wrote those letters to her. Originally, I thought it might be Mrs. Mulberry and her group. But they seemed genuinely as shocked as we are about it. And Mrs. Mulberry is very agreeable. I just never thought she was that good of a stage actor. It just makes me curious who it could be."

Big John shrugged and his expression turned thoughtful again. "I believe, that whoever it is, their intentions are for the best. From what I'm seeing, there's no malice there, just good intentions."

"I agree with you. This town needs a little reviving with young couples to bring children into this world and into our community. There is no denying women make life better. Take the sheriff into account. Have you seen his yard lately? There are flowers blooming where before it was just mostly drabness. And on the inside, it's bright and cheery with colorful pillows she and Janie have made. And that little girl is thriving." It was all true.

The older man nodded with a serious expression and a smile. "I believe you are talking yourself into something. I totally agree with you."

Jarred took a deep breath and contemplated the blue sky for a moment. It suddenly seemed brighter as he remembered the kiss he and Gabby shared. "Big John, I do believe I might be in love." He stopped speaking as he let the words run through him. And clarity settled in. "And I'm grateful, really grateful to whoever wrote the letter. Now I just need to hope the Lord helps me, and Gabby can fall for me. Before she decides to leave."

Big John clapped him on the shoulder. "I'll pray for you. Surely after all this she's not going to leave."

A few moments later, he said good-bye to Big John and headed down to the livery stable, where he dropped off the buggy and horse. He prayed all the way that Gabby would stay.

Surely since she had kissed him so sweetly, it was a sign that she was drawn to him.

Then again, there was the other dilemma: she didn't think she was cut out to be a pastor's wife. And that might prove to be his biggest obstacle to overcome.

CHAPTER TEN

The days that followed were some of the best that Gabby had ever felt. She grew stronger every day. Mrs. Mulberry had not been blind; she had known the moment Gabby had walked into the house that something wonderful had happened. She was definitely a romantic heart, as was Essie Jane. The two older ladies had the best time when they got together and she thought, when she heard them giggling in the next room three days after the buggy ride, that they might very well be happily planning her marriage. It was a bit unsettling.

The problem with all the happiness she'd felt the last few days—and despite how much she'd enjoyed him coming by to sit with her on the swing in the evenings—was she feared she was not cut out to be a pastor's wife. That feeling would not leave her.

And she told the two older ladies. Of course, they both told her that was a ridiculous assumption. But it was a true and valid fear that she had. And no one, including Lucy, believed her. Lucy also was completely thrilled about the situation and had not hidden her excitement when she had come to visit yesterday. There was also no denying that Lucy was totally and completely in love with the sheriff despite the fact that she had not known that the person she was communicating with hadn't been the sheriff before she had come here to get married. Still, she couldn't convince Gabby wholeheartedly that was a possibility for her. Not when she worried so about her ability to be a pastor's wife.

She was in trouble because she knew she had fallen hard for Jarred. The doctor came to check on her and told her she was on the mend well enough to do what she felt like doing. This was great because she was anxious to find a job.

She and Mrs. Mulberry were walking out of the house to head to town when Jarred came by, riding a horse.

"Good morning." He smiled down at them. "I wanted to stop by and say that I'm heading out to the Cross family this morning. Mr. Cross is having trouble with his back and unable to get his plowing done and Mrs. Cross isn't in the best of health, so it makes it hard on them. I'll be out there for a few days helping out and wanted to let you know that I won't be over at least this evening and probably tomorrow evening."

"You are so good to do this," Mrs. Mulberry said. "Can we bring some dinner out this evening?"

Gabby nodded, happy to hear they might be able to help. "Yes, we can do that if you think it's okay." No wonder he had such hard muscles—the man might be a pastor but he did much physical work.

"That would be a great blessing if you could do that." He smiled at them and his eyes warmed when they touched her.

Gabby felt as though she might melt. "We will," she said.

"Yes, we will," Mrs. Mulberry agreed wholeheartedly.

He tipped his hat. "Then I'll see you then."

They watched him ride off and Gabby's heart rode with him.

"It's no wonder the man has such muscles. He does this sort of thing all the time. He doesn't just talk about helping people—he does it. Filling in for people who need him."

Gabby found that she loved that about him. Loved the kindness of him and the giving spirit that he had, that he was truly a man who didn't just talk it but walked with the Lord. He was a man of action.

He was well loved by everyone and with reason, it seemed.

Though they had only known each other for little more than a week, she had fallen for him. Not just fallen for him but had fallen for everything about him.

And at night, when she lay down to sleep, memories of his kiss kept her awake. She longed for more.

Essie Jane came over and they all started cooking after lunch. They planned several meals to take out to the Cross family. Gabby loved working with the two ladies to help the family.

"I love what you two ladies stand for." Gabby paused in making cornbread to smile at the two sweet ladies who had helped her through her own trying time. "You both helped me and now you're helping others."

"So are you," Essie Jane said. "It's easy to help others. We are glad to have you helping. And I'm sure your young man is happy to have you help too."

Her young man. Gabby thought of Jarred and the idea that they were calling him hers was disconcerting. She knew she loved him but that didn't mean she would let herself move past that. Too many things stood in her way. She hadn't yet sent her father a letter because she was so uncertain about what she wanted to do. No, she had thought deeply and long over the last three days, trying to decide what she wanted to do.

Mrs. Mulberry had assured her she was welcome as long as she wanted to stay. That gave her time to make plans for her future. A future that she determined.

"We don't want you to leave," Mrs. Mulberry said.

Essie Jane smiled. "We don't. We have a plan."

Gabby stared at them and knew that these two sweet ladies wanted her to stay very much.

"Okay, I'm staying. I decided that I shall write my father. He needs to know I am fine. I know that he and my mother are worried sick. I didn't want to write him until I knew what I wanted to do. And if I can find a way to support myself, I want to stay. I want to at least give myself a chance to make it here in this wonderful area with my two new friends. That's okay with you two?"

In answer, both women came and wrapped her arms around her and they all hugged in one giant ball.

Mrs. Mulberry backed up after a second. "So are

you considering pursuing Pastor Andrews?"

Gabby felt herself blush. "My heart tells me to. But I'm still uncertain about being a pastor's wife." She smiled. "I'll just have to see where we go. If he feels the same way, then we may move cautiously. But he is so amazing. He needs an amazing spouse."

Mrs. Mulberry frowned. "And why do you not think you are amazing? You were completely ready to help with this meal."

She could talk all she wanted to but that didn't help calm the fear inside Gabby. She had never been called on to give much of herself all of her life. It was just not something her mother or her father had instilled in them. They had been a part of the affluent class, on the lower edges of it, but her mother had always taken pride in who they were. That, in part, was much of Gabby's decision to take the train ticket and stage and find her own way. Something inside her wanted a different life. A life that meant something more. But was she good enough? She needed to make it on her own...to find out who she really was.

Essie Jane clasped her hands together. "Oh my word, this is so exciting. We have a new romance. I can't wait for you to come to church on Sunday. It will be a grand day for you to be there. Pastor Andrews is a wonderful speaker, teacher, and a blessing to our community. I just can't help but want the best for him. And I do believe that is you."

Mrs. Mulberry nodded excitedly. "I agree, I agree wholeheartedly. And now Essie Jane and I have a proposal for you."

The two ladies exchanged glances and then beamed at Gabby. Gabby's nerves rattled with uncertainty of what these two had come up with now.

"We have decided that we are bored. And we know you are wanting a job. So we were thinking that there was an opportunity for us to be a blessing in other ways with our baking skills. We wondered if maybe you would be willing or want to open a bakery with us? Do you think that people would pay for my scones and the sweet treats that we love to bake?"

Essie Jane looked as if she were holding her

breath. Now, she spoke in a rush. "We have the most wonderful time baking together. And it would give you an income. While it would give us an outlet to bring in income for ourselves also."

Tears pricked Gabby's eyes. These two were amazing. "That is the most wonderful idea. Yes, people would clamor to buy your baked goods. They would probably come from all over."

Mrs. Mulberry beamed. "Now I wouldn't go that far with praise." She chuckled.

"They might," Gabby said. "You said yourself that women are scarce. These men love something fresh baked. Of course, I'm not much of a baker but I can help do other things. I have a willing heart and am happy to learn. But are you sure?"

Both ladies scowled. "Of course we're serious," Essie Jane said.

"We are so excited," Mrs. Mulberry added. "The very idea of having my own business… I just can't even express how exciting that is for me."

Gabby was too, more than she could express.

"What a great adventure this will be."

Jarred was worn out by the time he rode his horse back into town the next afternoon. The ladies had come out and brought the Cross family enough food to last them a week and he'd been so proud to see how much Gabby enjoyed talking to the older couple. She had been a breath of fresh air to them and she'd seemed, as her companions had, very excited. They'd left before nightfall so they would make it back before dark and he'd gone to the barn to sleep and dream of Gabby. Today he'd plowed the rest of the field and found himself missing Gabby more than he'd ever missed anyone.

Thinking of her had been the bright spot of his day.

And he'd managed to make it home before dark, so maybe she would be waiting for him on Mrs. Mulberry's porch swing.

He hoped so. He wanted her in every sense of the word. He wanted her for his wife; he wanted her as a husband would want his wife and as a partner longing for a lifetime friend. Jarred wanted Gabby, and he wanted to be everything she wanted him to be in her life.

He just prayed that she would realize that she was everything he needed in a wife. Love was the first ingredient to the mix and he had an abundance of that for her.

God had brought her this far; he just prayed that it would work. He walked up the path. His heart thundered as she stood up to greet him.

"I'm so glad you made it." She came toward him and into his arms. "I assume you finished the plowing."

"I did. And I'm glad to be here holding you." His heart swelled with love as his arms tightened around her and he kissed the top of her head. "I could get used to this, you know."

She looked up at him. "Me too."

Her words seeped through him like warm sunshine. "Gabby, I need to tell you how I feel for you. I know God worked a miracle bringing you into my life in the way that He got you here."

"I think so too."

"Would you like to take a ride?"

"I would love that."

The sun was settling in the sky as they took a short ride not too far outside of town to a beautiful, bluebonnet covered piece of land. In the dusk, it was about as romantic a spot as he'd ever seen. He hoped Gabby liked it. He pulled the wagon to a halt and secured the leathers.

"Oh Jarred, what a beautiful spot."

"I think so. I know it's dusk and we'll have to hurry back to town but I wanted to show this to you." He hopped from the wagon and hurried around to hold a hand up to her. She smiled at him and his heart thundered as she took his hand.

"You seem so excited." She held his hand and stepped from the carriage.

They stood so close and it was all he could do not to wrap her in his arms and pull her closer. "I am. I was granted this piece of property from a wealthy member of the church before he passed away a few years ago. He told me it was for when I was ready to start a family. The parsonage is so tiny. He said he wanted to go to heaven knowing the Lord was happy with him by doing right by his preacher."

"That is so touching." Her voice quivered.

He took her hands in his. "I was blessed to know him and was overcome by his generosity. I thought that it would be a perfect place to build a home one day...when I had a wife and was ready to have children." He went down on one knee. "Gabby, will you marry me? I love you and I don't want to even think about a day when you're not in my life. I'm praying you'll do me the great honor and become my wife."

Gabby could not believe her ears. Or her eyes. Jarred was on his knees, looking up at her in a way that caused her to melt inside. Her plans, everything she'd believed when she'd made this trip out West, had altered from how she'd perceived it would be. She had fallen in love with the man before her. It had happened so quickly that her head was practically spinning.

"Jarred, I am overwhelmed by your words. And to be honest, I do want to accept. I love you, I do, but—" Her words were barely out when he rose from his knees, swept her into his arms and his lips covered hers.

Moments passed but she had no recollection of them as all she could think about was the blessed feel of his lips on hers and the solid feel of his body pressed against hers. She might faint with sheer delight and passion was all her mind could comprehend.

When he pulled away and gazed with passion-glazed eyes into hers, she felt as if she were jam heated by the hot summer sun. Her pulse pounded against her temple and she thought surely he could hear it.

When at last she was able to break the kiss, she forced the words from her lips. "But Jarred, I'm still afraid I don't have what it takes to be your wife."

"You will be an excellent pastor's wife. But more importantly, you'll be my wonderful wife. You're good-hearted and kind and you love the Lord. Those are qualities that qualify you. Unless you do not love me and do not want to be a pastor's wife, then nothing stands in your way. I want you with all my heart."

She could not say no. Could not deny her heart what it wanted. "Yes, then, I will marry you. And be glad of it. But I'm planning to open a bakery business with Mrs. Mulberry and Essie Jane. I still want to do that."

He nuzzled her neck, sending shivers of delight coursing through her.

"You have my blessing. As long as I get first dibs on your heart and the cherry scones."

She laughed and hugged him tight. "Yes to everything. I love you, Jarred Andrews, and cannot wait to be Mrs. Andrews."

EPILOGUE

They were married the next day by Sheriff Jones, right after Jarred ended a very enthusiastic sermon to a full church. If she'd been afraid she wouldn't be welcomed, Gabby had been mistaken. Her life was forever changed and she was welcomed into the town and congregation with open arms.

Lucy, Ambrosia, and Essie Jane had all joined together and given them a wedding dinner and reception afterwards. And that night, she and Jarred had joined their hearts and souls together in the most beautiful way. Gabby thanked God for working behind the scenes to bring them together in the most unusual way that he had. She, from runaway bride to mail-order bride to preacher's wife…it was a miracle.

And if that wasn't blessing enough, the bakery was a roaring success. Cowboys, farmers, and families came from all over the county to celebrate today's opening day, two weeks after Gabby's wedding. But true to her word, she boxed a dozen cherry scones and presented them to Jarred with a kiss. Love was the sweetest treat of all.

Jarred was the happiest man alive as he left the Sweet Shop with his box of scones…but it was the kiss from his wife that had him smiling as he ran into Big John.

"Well, preacher, you're smiling mighty big there. You look about as happy as a squirrel in a barrel of acorns."

Jarred laughed. "That describes how I feel completely. I tell you, Big John, I have been blessed beyond my imagination and other than the good Lord, I don't know who to thank."

"Oh really, what do you mean?"

"The matchmaker. I still have no idea who brought Gabby here, or I should say, who tried to bring the other young lady here for me. But it ended up God took over and brought me Gabby. If I knew who it was, I'd thank her from the bottom of my heart."

Big John crossed his arms over his wide chest and rubbed his jaw with his fingers. "I'm sure whoever it was probably has been watching and can see your thankfulness in that smile of yours. It's beaming brighter than the sun, so I'm sure I'm not the only one who sees it."

Jarred nodded. "I'm sure you're right. I've made no attempt to hide my happiness nor the fact that a matchmaker brought me and Gabby together…with a helping hand from the Lord. I'll be getting several sermons from that idea and how God truly does work in mysterious ways."

"I think that's a great idea."

"I look around and see men all the time who I think could benefit from a matchup like mine. For instance, look down there at Sam McKay. He lives all the way out there on the edge of the county and every time I see him, I can't help thinking he needs a wife."

Sam was crossing the street, headed toward the bakery with long strides and a frown. The man wore serious on his face like it was a permanent expression.

"You know, I was thinking the same thing. Just yesterday, when I dropped by the bakery to bring Ambrosia one of my Millie's baking dishes to use in the store, Ambrosia said the same thing to me. Said he was one of the fellas she often made scones for, like she did you and for me. And that she wondered who the matchmaker was and wished whoever it was would bring someone to town for Sam."

"Isn't that interesting," Jarred said, as Sam stepped into the line of men waiting to get into the bakery.

"That's what I thought. I figured if she was thinking that and you and I were thinking the same thing—that maybe the matchmaker might have sights on him too. We'll just have to wait and see."

Jarred laughed. "I guess you're right. Come to think of it, look at that whole line of men waiting for something sweet…what they all need is something sweet like the Lord brought me. I think I'll start praying for them to be blessed like I was."

Big John grinned. "I think that whoever the matchmaker is would appreciate that, Pastor."

"You take care, Big John. I'm heading home to have a scone and a cup of coffee before I start preparing my sermon." With that, Jarred stepped off the sidewalk and headed toward the parsonage. His steps were light and his heart danced with happiness. He'd say those prayers, and brush up on reciting the wedding vows because something told him someone else was soon going to ask him to perform a wedding…he just had to wait and see who the next lucky bachelor would be.

Big John was all smiles as he crossed the street to his feed store. As he entered the building, he pulled a folded letter from his pocket and smiled. One of the lonesome cowboys he'd secretly written a letter for had received a reply…and he couldn't wait to see which one was getting the next mail-order bride. Yup, his Millie, bless her dear heart, would have enjoyed this so much. He couldn't help but think she was up there giving the good Lord a helping hand.

"Yes, Millie my love, two perfect matches and more to come."

Don't miss Elizabeth Chase's clean and wholesome novel, THE RANCHER'S MAIL-ORDER BRIDE, book 3 in her exciting Mail-Order Brides of Sweet, Texas. You'll love this clean and wholesome mail order bride historical western romance series.

Excerpt from

THE RANCHER'S MAIL-ORDER BRIDE

Mail-Order Brides of Sweet, Texas Book Three

CHAPTER ONE

Sam McKay was tired of having to buy baked goods at the new bakery in town. He was grateful that three ladies in town had opened the bakery recently. Their delicious pastries and pies helped him satisfy his sweet tooth since he had no wife to bake them for him and he didn't wish to have one. At least, there hadn't been a wish before. Lately, he'd begun feeling restless and unsatisfied in many other aspects of his life. He'd begun to wish for more in his life…

More comforts in his home.

More baked goods. He'd begun to wish for the scent of warm bread baking in the oven and fresh apple pies cooling on the counter. He'd had a dream recently of a sweet-scented woman waiting for him when he came in from the fields. She had a dusting of flour and sugar on her cheek and he'd kissed it off the moment he'd walked into the house.

Like a bandit in the night, the thought slammed into him and he tried to force it away with a determined kick.

But it had grabbed hold like a cowboy determined not to get thrown by a wild horse.

There had to be more to life than just working from sunrise to sunset. He knew there was; he'd witnessed it in others. Like the preacher and the sheriff, who'd both recently married and had a joy shining in their eyes that he envied. That contentment that was obvious now stirred this new dissatisfaction he was experiencing.

He wanted more joy in his life.

But it was a fantasy. He worked from daylight till dark and it wasn't fair to bring a woman all the way out here and leave her stranded during the day while he worked.

He and his younger brother, Gil had been working the family ranch alone for the last couple of years since losing their parents to a bad fever. He knew firsthand that life out West was hard and unforgiving.

He'd dealt with their deaths the only way he'd known how; he'd thrown himself into continuing their dream of building the ranch. It was lonesome out here. The ride into town took about four hours and he didn't go into town unless he had to because it took him away from his chores for too long. But he would have to go this week.

Standing beside the fence, he wiped sweat from his brow and stared out across the expanse of pasture to watch as Chauncey Todd, the old miner, who had a small camp at the corner of Sam's ranch, rode toward him on his mule, Tidbit.

"A mighty fine mornin' to ya, Sam," Chauncey called, then spat a stream of tobacco out and grinned widely.

Sam studied the man and his uncharacteristic good humor. "What's got you smiling this morning? Did you hit gold?"

The grizzled man grinned wider as his mule stopped in front of Sam. "Naw, jest got a message fer you from Big John Wiggins at the feed store. Since I was on my way back from town, he asked me to deliver it to you. It's about the stagecoach that's arriving tomorrow." He scratched his scraggly beard. "Looks like important business."

"Did you order something?" Gil asked. Excitement lit his face.

"No." Sam frowned. "I don't have any business with the stagecoach."

The feed store that Big John owned was the official stage stop in town. If there were messages that needed forwarding from passengers of the stagecoach, they sent them through telegraphs in care of Big John. But Sam had no business with the stage.

Chauncey spat tobacco. "I'm jest delivering the envelope with the message in it." He held it out.

"Go on, read it," Gil urged.

Sam took it and stared at the front, then turned it over and studied the back.

"Well, don't just stare at it." Gil moved closer.

He shot his little brother a glare then opened the envelope and pulled the page from inside.

Sam McKay your mail-order bride, Miss. Megan Scott, will be arriving on the stagecoach tomorrow and will need you to pick her up.

Sam scowled in disbelief at the letter, then at Chauncey. "*Who* sent this?"

"Big John. He said it was urgent. Said he found the note slipped under the door when he opened the store this morning. Said he was just passing the message on so the poor woman wasn't left standing alone in front of his store. Said it was *ur*-gent. What else does it say that makes you turn so green?"

"It says *my* mail-order bride is arriving tomorrow."

Gil's jaw dropped. "You ordered a *mail-order bride*?"

"We been wonderin' who was gonna get the next

one." Chauncey's grin widened. "You going to go get her?"

Sam's eyes narrowed and he glared at his brother and Chauncey. "I didn't order a mail-order bride. This has to be a joke."

"I bet it ain't. The sheriff and the preacher both done got themselves a mail-order bride and neither one of them ordered one either. But, they sure are happy. And I, fer one, am too. That there is one good bakery the preacher's bride opened with Ambrosia Mulberry and Essie Jane Tate. I got me a bag of goodies right thar in my saddlebag. It looks like tomorrow is gonna be your lucky day."

Gil was nodding like a tree limb caught in a tornado at Chauncey's longwinded declaration. "It's true and you know it, Sam."

Anger drew his brows together. "This is not right. Who in this town is luring these women here? I'm going to town, and if this poor woman really is on that stage, I'm sending her back home. This is cruel, tricking these women like this."

Chauncey looked puzzled. "The preacher and the

sheriff's wives don't seem to think it was cruel. Seems like they're real happy. They're both smiling. And the sheriff's little daughter is all happy now that she's got her a mama. And like I said, me and you and all the men folks in town are happy about the bakery going in. So, it jest don't seem cruel at all to me."

"I agree with Chauncey. Think about it, Sam. We could get us some good meals cooked in the evenings. We wouldn't have to eat so many beans."

That was tempting. Sam took a slow breath and tried to calm his temper. He did like the bakery like Gil said but it wasn't enough to let the ridiculousness of this letter overtake his good sense. They didn't get treats often and that bakery was like heaven when they did get to town. But still that didn't change the fact that some poor female was about to find out that she didn't have a groom waiting on her.

He thought about it and another truth hit his conscience. He growled with frustration and stared down at the letter, his thoughts churning. "The one thing I can't do is have her getting off the stage thinking she's meeting me and no one be there to meet her. Not after she's already been lured out here by someone posing as me." He gritted his jaw then sighed. "So, I guess I'm going to have to go in to town and meet her. And then tell her the truth."

Chauncey crossed his arms and spat another long stream of tobacco. "I'm thinkin' tomorrow is going to be an interestin' day to be in town. I might jest load up and go back just to see you meet your new bride. You sure yer goin' to send her packin'? You seem lonely out here."

"I am sending her packing and I'm fine. You live all the way out here and you're okay."

Chauncey looked undeterred. "I'm an old geezer. But you're a right young man and you need a wife. Maybe this matchmaker in Sweet knows this. I been watchin' and it looks to me like whoever it is pretending to be you fellas and luring these pretty ladies out here ain't doing it carelessly. Seems to me, whoever it is is picking you out carefully."

Sam might have thought that about the sheriff and the preacher but why him? "I don't care what their reasoning is. I can find my own wife when I'm good and ready," he grunted.

"If that's so, then where is she?" Gil asked, defiant.

Chauncey scratched his whiskered jaw. "Yep, where you gonna find her? There ain't no young women in our little town. Sweet's got cowboys and sodbusters, but unless you're able to see something I can't see, then where exactly you goin' to find this bride? If I was you, I wouldn't be too hasty in turning her away."

"He's right. This might be your last chance, Sam."

"Yer brother might be right." Chauncey grinned and then, without another word, he turned Tidbit and tromped off down the road, whistling as he went.

He watched the old man riding away then he shot Gil a glare. "Don't you have chores to tend to?"

Gil huffed an exasperated breath. "Don't let her get away. Remember, I benefit from this too."

"If you know what's good for you, then you'd better get back to work. This is my life this matchmaker is playing with and I'll not have it."

"Fine." Gil spun and stomped off, his shoulders

stiff.

Sam reread the letter.

How had this happened? Who was it who thought he needed a wife? It was true he'd been thinking about the idea of a wife but then he'd talk himself out of it. But to think that someone in town had taken it upon themselves to send for a wife for him was unacceptable.

He wasn't a charity case and he could make his own decisions. He thought about what Chauncey had pointed out and it was true; he did get lonesome out here. His brother lived across the pasture in his small cabin and worked the ranch right along beside him, so he had company.

A wife was different, though, and the thought churned inside him. *A wife would be nice.*

But not a mail-order bride who someone else had picked out for him. Nope, he wasn't standing for that. He would go to town and he would send the poor woman back where she came from. And if he had to resort to sending for his own mail-order bride, he would. But he would be in control of who he sent for and not some anonymous matchmaker.

Who was the matchmaker anyway? There was speculation that the church ladies might be responsible. He hadn't really given it much thought, until now, because he'd had no idea he would be a target.

Later, as he lay in bed that night, tired and worn out from building a fence and digging out the creek, he wondered about the woman he would meet at the stage in the morning.

The woman who had braved the rugged trip across Texas to marry a stranger.

The woman he was going to turn away. The thought dug at him.

Books in the Mail-Order Brides of Sweet, Texas

About the Author

Elizabeth Chasen loves to write 'hopeful' romantic stories that inspire and entertain. All of her books are clean and wholesome Christian romance. She finds joy in bringing her fun characters to life and giving each of her couples their happy ending!

Always fascinated by Mail Order Bride historical romance, she enjoys creating her own stories to bring to her readers. Mail Order Brides of Sweet, Texas is the first of many series to come, so enjoy and she invites you to join her mailing list so you'll be the first to hear when her next exciting historical western romance is releasing. Just go to:

ww.elizabethchasen.blogspot.com. Happy reading!

www.ingramcontent.com/pod-product-compliance
Lightning Source LLC
Chambersburg PA
CBHW070338130626
46556CB00007B/2919